Straw Sense

Straw Sense

BY RONA RUPERT

ILLUSTRATED BY
MIKE DOOLING

SIMON & SCHUSTER BOOKS FOR YOUNG READERS
Published by Simon & Schuster
New York London Toronto Sydney Tokyo Singapore

jε

SIMON & SCHUSTER BOOKS FOR YOUNG READERS
Simon & Schuster Building, Rockefeller Center
1230 Avenue of the Americas, New York, New York 10020.
Text copyright © 1993 by Rona Rupert.
Illustrations copyright © 1993 by Mike Dooling.
SIMON & SCHUSTER BOOKS FOR YOUNG READERS
is a trademark of Simon & Schuster.
Designed by Vicki Kalajian.
The text of this book is set in 15 pt. ITC Berkeley Old Style Medium.
The display type is Bernhard Modern Bold.
The Illustrations were done as oil paintings.
Manufactured in the United States of America

10 9 8 7 6 5 4 3 2 1

Library of Congress Cataloging-in-Publication Data
Rupert, Rona. Straw sense / by Rona Rupert ;
illustrated by Mike Dooling.
Summary: An old man who makes dolls breaks through
the loneliness of a young boy who doesn't speak.
[1. Mutism, Elective—Fiction.   2. Dolls—Fiction.
3. Friendship—Fiction.]   I. Dooling, Michael, ill.   II. Title.
PZ7.R8885St 1993 [E]—dc20 CIP 92-8775
ISBN 0-671-77047-0

*For all the children
who have been charmed by the
strawberry people*

RR

*To my family for their support:
Mom, Grams, Jane, Rachel, Lisa,
Steve, Tom, Lynn*

MD

He never spoke. When asked a question, he answered only if he could do so by moving his head. Yes or no—he would move his head up and down, or from side to side.

"There's nothing wrong with him," said the woman with whom he stayed. "He lost his voice the night the forest burned down," she said, "but there is nothing wrong with his head."

That was her way of saying that he was as bright as anybody else. And nobody argued, because there was no one who knew them well enough to say whether it was so or not. They were newcomers who had moved to the strawberry fields just before the winter had started.

But, to prove that what she had said was true, Shamiema, the woman who called herself his aunt, gave him money and sent him to the roadside stall to buy new potatoes and tomatoes.

"And bring back the change," she said.

He nodded and left.

It rained—the cold, drizzly kind of rain that falls early in spring. The ditch he had to cross to get to the road was overgrown with reeds. Hanging onto the strong green leaves, he waded ankle-deep through the mud.

Before taking on the wide, tarred road, he stopped at the mimosa tree to inspect the weaverbirds' nests that hung from its branches. It was then that he noticed the open door of the shed on the other side of the road. It was as though it was beckoning him.

The rain came down even harder than before, so he carefully crossed the wet road and approached the shed.

He stepped into the shelter of the dark entrance and waited quietly with his back turned to whatever was inside. He listened to the movement behind him until he could no longer bear not knowing. Then slowly he turned his head.

Whether the old man knew about him he couldn't tell, for the man did not look his way. He was working on some kind of doll. It was as big as himself, and the man was dressing it in what looked like his own clothes: a pair of white pants and a white shirt. The sleeves of the shirt were too long for the doll's arms, and he had to roll them up. Then he patiently fastened the front buttons. The doll had no feet or hands. The old man put a kind of hat on its head, and then he laid it down on the rough wooden worktable.

"Lie still," he said. "I have to work on your face."

This he did with his back to the boy, whose name was Goolam-Habib, although no one knew it. Nor did anybody know that his surname was Tofie, pronounced exactly like the name of the candy.

Goolam-Habib leaned forward to see what the old man was doing. He had learned to move as quietly as a cat.

"Eyes to see with," the old man said.

Goolam-Habib stretched his neck. He saw the two pink half-moon eyes the old man had sewed onto the high forehead of the doll.

When he had finished, he put a patch of blue cloth onto the middle of the face. "A nose to smell with," he said.

The mouth was large and red.

"A mouth to talk with," he said.

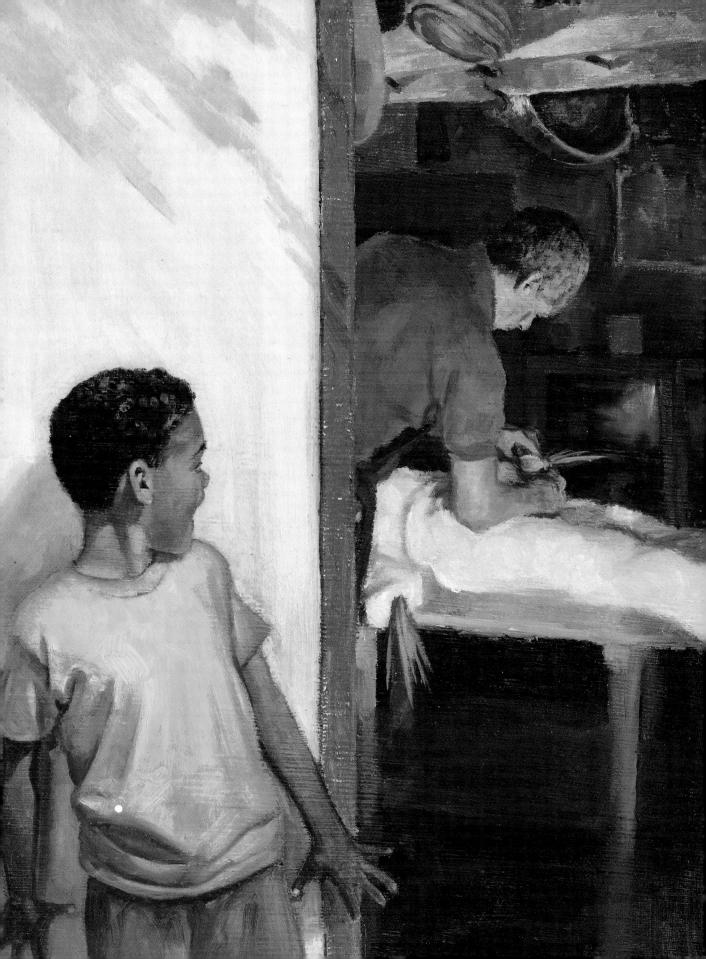

This reminded Goolam-Habib of Shamiema. He left as quietly as he had come, still not knowing whether the old man knew he was there or not.

When he came to the stall, he pointed to the potatoes and the tomatoes, and nodded his head. He gave the fat woman who sold them the money. He counted the change, and he nodded his head again to tell her that the change she had given him was correct.

He skipped a few times as he crossed the tarred road beside which the steam was now rising. The sun had suddenly appeared and was shining hot, and there was a rainbow. He deliberately did not turn his head in the direction of the shed.

"See!" said Shamiema happily to her neighbors when he delivered the vegetables. "Everything exactly as I wanted it, and he isn't six yet."

They nodded and continued hanging up the wash. They were glad to get it out of their houses.

Goolam-Habib looked at the clothing and sheets and towels on the line. He loved the way the wind blew them forward and backward and sometimes right over. He looked beyond the washing to the neat rows of strawberry plants. They were covered with white flowers. He tried to see the shed where the old man was working on the doll but could not.

Not seeing it did not stop him from thinking about it, though. He had the feeling that the old man and his doll had moved right into his head.

The next morning he slipped away as soon as he could manage, taking another route to the road. It was a footpath that bordered the big strawberry field. From there it passed the vlei where the women picked waterblommetjies. They tied them in bunches and sold them to the people

who passed in their cars. Goolam-Habib made himself
small, hoping that nobody would notice him. Nobody did.

He crossed the tarred road and went straight to the shed.
The weaverbirds were making noises in the trees as he
stepped into the doorway.

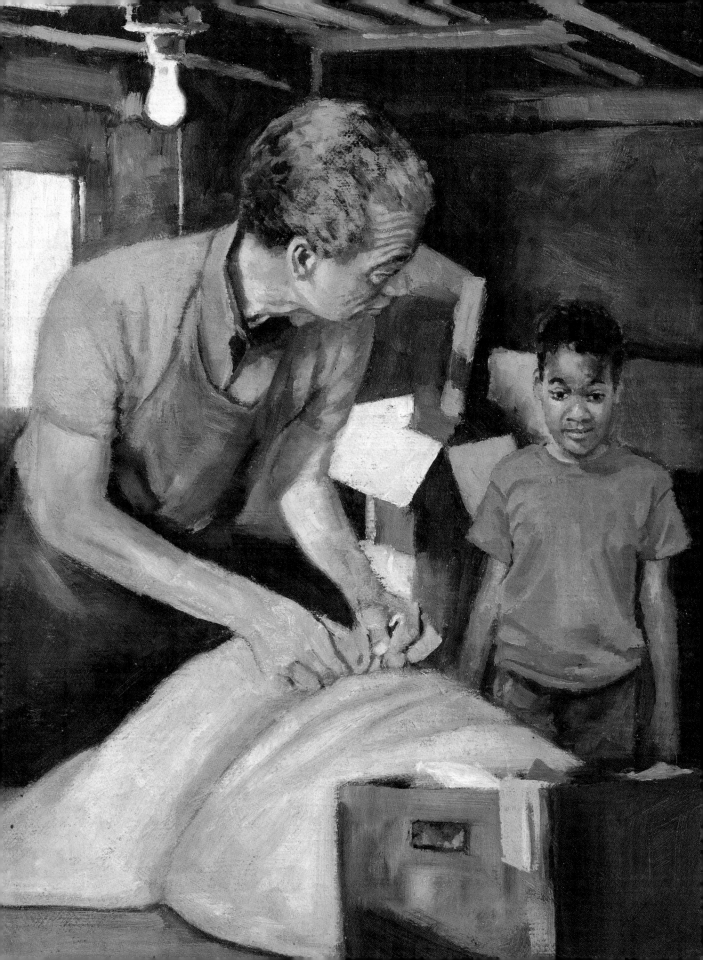

"There you are," said the old man. "Can you give me a hand?"

Goolam-Habib swallowed and moved forward. He was so scared he could not think of doing anything else.

"Here," said the old man. "I need someone to help me stick feathers onto the ostrich. The doll wants something to sit on outside."

Goolam-Habib turned his eyes in the direction of the old man's crooked finger. Outside, between two rows in the strawberry patch, the doll sat, propped up against a stone. He looks sad, Goolam-Habib thought.

"He has to scare away the birds," said the old man. "The strawberries are ready for picking."

The old man was gluing little pieces of material onto the body of a big, long-necked bird-doll.

"You can start at the front," he said to Goolam-Habib, who quickly caught on.

They worked hard. Before lunchtime the ostrich was out in the strawberry field, the doll sitting on top of it and holding it tightly around its long neck.

"Thank you," said the old man. "I appreciate your help. Without it I still would have been working."

Goolam-Habib caught himself humming as he skipped back to the house in which he and Shamiema and her husband, Rashaad, were living. He found a spot in the backyard on top of the woodpile from where he could see the doll straddling the ostrich, and he watched him as often as he could. He knew that this pleased Shamiema, as she did not like him upsetting anything inside the house. And she liked it when he was quiet.

Then the rains came back.

"It makes you wonder," said Shamiema, "about that old man Noah and his ark."

Goolam-Habib often thought about the doll chasing away the birds. What did *he* do in the rain? There was no way he could find out, for Shamiema would not allow him out of the house, not even out of the kitchen, for she did not like muddy footprints on her shiny floors.

After two days the sun was back. He sneaked out and climbed onto the woodpile and looked.

What he saw were two dolls and an ostrich. The second doll was standing right next to the first.

He did not even bother to ask Shamiema if he could go, he just ran. The old man was at the door. Goolam-Habib had the feeling that he was expecting him.

"He was lonely," he said, "so I made him a wife."

Goolam-Habib went round the house to the strawberry field. There they were: the man-doll on the ostrich and his wife. She wore a pink polka-dot blouse and an apron with a huge pocket in the front. Her face was yellow, and she had blue eyes and a blue nose and a blue mouth.

"And now *she* starts complaining," said the old man.

Goolam-Habib looked at him.

"She wants a child. Will you help me make her one?"

Goolam-Habib nodded his head.

"I thought you would. It is no good having an unhappy scarecrow in your strawberry field."

They started right away. This was the first time Goolam-
Habib worked on a doll from the beginning. He helped the
old man stuff straw into the body and the arms and legs,
and tie up the ends.

Her arms were green.

There was another pink polka-dot blouse in the bag in
which the rags were kept. Goolam-Habib pulled it out.

"You like it?" the old man asked.

Goolam-Habib nodded.

"Go on, help her get dressed then," the old man said,
and Goolam-Habib did.

She had a beautiful dark blue face, and her eyes were
white. Her nose was pink, and her mouth was green.

When Goolam-Habib left—only because he knew
Shamiema would start looking for him soon—the old man
was braiding her hair. It was made of strips of red and
white cloth.

"Don't stay away too long," he said to Goolam-Habib.
"She'll miss you."

Goolam-Habib smiled and waved and ran all the way
home. He was happy to find that no one had started to
look for him.

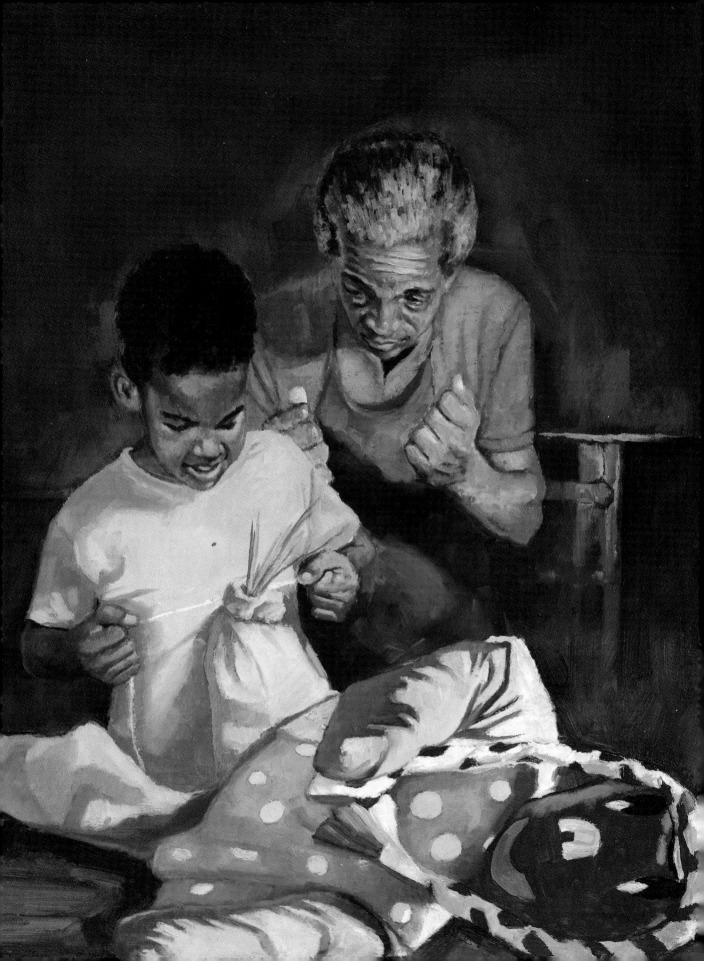

He had hardly woken up the next morning when Shamiema said, "Today I'm going to the village to buy supplies. Are you coming along?"

Goolam-Habib's heart almost stopped beating. He shook his head violently.

"Don't get so upset," she said. "I'm only asking."

After she left, he took the road to the shed, running all the way. The door was open, but the old man was not inside. Goolam-Habib ran round the house and was stopped in his tracks by what he saw.

The blue girl with the braids was riding a red bicycle. Her head was tilted toward him. She was way in front of her mother and father, and was coming his way, smiling at him. He thought he saw her move her arm, and he waved back at her.

The old man was near her, working on the strawberries.

He stood up when he saw Goolam-Habib, and he beckoned to him to come closer. "Let me introduce you," he said. "Daisy, this is..." He looked at Goolam-Habib.

Goolam-Habib looked at all the faces—at the father's and the mother's, at the beautiful blue girl's, at the old man's— and he saw that the sadness had gone from them. He knew why. Like them, he, too, was no longer lonely.

So he smiled and he turned to the girl-doll on the bicycle. "Goolam-Habib," he said. "My name is Goolam-Habib."

"Goolam-Habib," he said again.

The old man touched his shoulder briefly. "We are pleased to meet you," he said. "Goolam-Habib, what a nice name. Call me Saul."

And Goolam-Habib said clearly, "Pleased to meet you, Saul."